The Big Idea Notebook for Kids

INVENTING

T. Sumner

Copyright © 2011, T. Sumner

All rights reserved. No part of this book may be reproduced, stored, or transmitted by any means—whether auditory, graphic, mechanical, or electronic—without written permission of both publisher and author. Unauthorized reproduction of any part of this work is illegal and is punishable by law.

ISBN 978-1-105-16001-1

Contents

For my Mom and all kids like me who want to be an inventor.

Preface

The Big Idea Notebook for Kids is a series of books designed to teach kids about the very basics of specific subjects written in easy-to-understand language. This book will not only teach you the very basics of Inventing and how fun it is to do, but provides a handy notebook so you can write down all your ideas and even draw them.

Foreword

Hi. My name is Taryn, I'm 10 years old and I want to be an inventor… well a doctor, an actress and an inventor. I made this book so that kids my age can start to learn about inventing and how fun it is!

I can't say that my inventions have made millions of dollars just yet, but they will! I have a lot of fun thinking of ideas and so can you. Anytime you come up with a game to play with your friends, that's an invention! Any time you play a board game and make up better rules, that's an invention! You can make an invention that changes a person's life for the better. I personally like to think up new ideas for pets. I have dogs.

This notebook is filled with things I've learned about inventing I think you should know. One of the first things I learned was to write down my ideas. That is why I made this invention notebook. Once you get an idea, all you have to do is write it down so you don't forget your idea.

My invention notebook also contains a story about "Sally and Bobby" and their adventures in inventing and a whole bunch of pages you can use to write down your ideas. Before you get to those parts, I want to tell you what I've learned about inventing. I hope you enjoy it.

Inventing is Fun

First of all, I just want you to know inventing is really fun. I think it's cool that you get to think of things that nobody else thought of. And just think - what if one day, just one day, your idea becomes a REAL product. Wouldn't that be really exciting? That would spread your name around. You'd also have you're very own company for your very own invention that nobody else thought of!

Don't Be Afraid

Don't be afraid if your invention seems outrageous or crazy. All inventions have a little spark to it that makes it have a bit of craziness. DO NOT be discouraged if somebody makes fun of your inventions.

Write in This Invention Notebook

ALWAYS write down your ideas in this notebook. You could also draw a picture of what the invention looks like. You can carry it around so when you go out and suddenly get an idea, you can jot it down.

Actually Do Something About Your Ideas

A lot of you must be thinking, I'm only a kid, how can I actually make an invention by myself? The answer to that is… DO NOT AND I MEAN DO NOT keep it to yourself! Tell an adult you can trust that can help you. Tell an adult that WOULDN'T tell anybody else that would steal your idea. Stealing an idea means when you tell somebody about your idea for an invention, and then they make it a real product and take credit for it. You'll learn more about stealing ideas later on.

Business Partners

Business partners are people who could help A LOT with your inventions. A business partner is somebody that helps you grow your business. You and your business partner would have to share a portion of money, depending on what you agree on. For example, if you agree you'd both get 50% of the money you get from your invention, you'd split the money in half between the two of you. You can have as many business partners as you want, but the best amount to have is 2-3 business partners. If your business partner does less work than you, it's not a good idea to split 50% of the profit.

Stealing Your Ideas

You must be very, very careful who you tell your ideas to! Only tell a parent or guardian about your idea or invention. Don't even tell a best friend! Make sure you write your invention in this notebook, with the date and sign it with your signature, and have your parent or guardian sign their signature too. If somebody steals your idea, you could get help by an adult and try to prove that you came up with the idea first.

Coming Up With a Name For Your Invention

Coming up with a name for an invention is easy - just be creative! And again, don't be worried if the name seems crazy or weird - that's the fun part of it! Just remember not to give your invention a boring name like, Jerry's first invention - the toy that is a bear. First of all, that's too long, and sounds boring! Give your invention a name like Jerry's Hairy Beary! Doesn't that sound much more exciting?

Decide What Inventions You'd Be Making

So the question is, "What inventions will you be making?" There are a lot of categories to choose from! Such as toys, pet products, food, electronics, and much more! The best one to choose is whichever you get the most ideas for and what interests you the most. You can make more than one type of invention if you want! It would be harder, but in the end, it would be worth it.

You Can Improve Existing Inventions

You can improve inventions that exist such as a sink or camera, but you might need to get permission. NEVER make an invention that you need permission for without actually getting permission. If you don't get permission for something that you need to get permission for, you could get in a lot of trouble.

How To Come Up With Ideas

Inventions come to me randomly or when I'm doing something related to it. Think about things that you like. Think about things that bug you, and try to come up with a way to resolve it. You could even come up with an idea when you're bored! Just think of what you wish was an invention and try to make it real!

Do You Even Want To Become An Inventor?

Do you even want to become an inventor? If you don't want to, you shouldn't! Nobody can force you to become an inventor. Inventing is really fun, and I'd recommend it. But it's totally up to you. You don't have to make an invention or even think of one if you don't want to.

Making Instructions

When you're finished with your invention, make sure you also type up some instructions! Without instructions, your invention won't be as successful. If you don't make instructions, some people won't know how to make, play, or use your invention.

Some inventions though, like a book, won't need instructions.

Warning Labels

Make sure you have a warning label for your product package

if it's needed! For example, if your invention has any small

pieces that little kids are capable of choking on or anything that

can damage your health, be sure to include a warning label. Make

the warning label say what you should be aware of and if you

should keep your invention away from children.

Picking Your Invention's Colors

When you're done coming up with your invention, make sure

it has some color! Pick some colors that look nice together. You

can make your invention have rainbow colors if you like! You

really can pick any color, just make sure it looks nice!

Packaging

If your invention is something you think that needs to be

packaged, come up with a good way to package it. If your inven-

tion is something like a sweatshirt, it could come in a plastic bag. If your invention is something that should come in a box, make the box look nice and appealing.

Packaging Attracts Buyers

Make the packaging for your invention look nice, not boring like an ordinary, brown box. Make it have some color, and some pictures. You could also put some words or sayings on the box such as what the invention is or what you can do with the invention.

Picking the Age Range

Pick an age range for your invention. If it's something that wouldn't be good for a little kid, put a sign on the packaging saying something such as "For ages as 8 and up." Or you can rate it "E," for everybody. If it's a toy, you don't have to pick an age range, unless the toy is for older kids.

Picking a Price for Your Invention

When you're finished with your invention, pick a price. Make sure the price is reasonable, and not overpriced. For example, if it's a stuffed animal, make sure it's only about $10, depending on its size.

You Can Make a Website for Your Invention

You can make a website for your invention. The website could let customers order your product or you can simply use your website to advertise your invention, or do anything you want! Just remember, you'll need an adult's help with making a website... So be sure to get help from a parent or trusted adult!

The Big Idea Notebook for Kids

INVENTING

1

Where Can I Find Ideas for an Invention?

SALLY AND HER FRIEND, BOBBY were talking one afternoon after school. They had been studying famous inventors like Alexander Graham Bell in class, so the idea of inventing was fresh on their minds.

"I think it would be cool to invent something and become famous," Sally said.

"That would be awesome," Bobby replied, "but what can we invent? I think everything has already been invented."

"Let's go see my Uncle Edward," Sally suggested, "He works for a company that makes new things all the time. Maybe he could tell us where to get ideas for an invention."

Uncle Edward was happy to see his niece and her friend, and he listened carefully to their explanation for dropping by that afternoon.

"Do you have to be an engineer or a scientist to be an inventor?" Bobby asked.

"Not at all. Anyone can become an inventor," Uncle Edward said.

"Well, if that means Bobby and I can be inventors, where can we get ideas?" Sally asked.

"Most ideas for inventions come from someone who recognizes a need for something new," Uncle Edward began. "Take the automobile, for example. Someone recognized a need to drive in the rain, so the windshield wiper was invented for that purpose. Later other improvements to the original windshield wiper were invented to make using them easier to use and more reliable."

"Oh, I see!" exclaimed Sally, "Ideas for inventions come from some kind of need like can openers to open canned food or hangers to put clothes in a closet."

"One famous inventor, Chester Greenwood, was only fifteen years old when he saw a need in 1873 and invented something still used today. In cold weather his cap protected his head and his coat collar protected his neck, but between the top of his head and neck, his ears got cold. His idea resulted in the invention of earmuffs," Uncle Edward told his young visitors.

"Are all inventions like that?" Bobby asked, "I mean for some practical use like earmuffs and can openers?"

"Not at all, Bobby," Uncle Edward replied, "People have invented things like board games and all sorts of toys like electric trains and model planes that really fly. Many inventions have been just to make our lives more enjoyable."

"Like television!" Sally exclaimed.

"Yes. And then other people began to find ways of making it better. When I was a boy we only had small black and white TVs until someone found a way to make them in full color. Now just look at all the inventions that have resulted in finding ways to use the TV for other purposes," Uncle Edward said.

"Like video games!" Bobby shouted.

It was time for Sally and Bobby to go home, but they left with a new excitement. They would start looking for a need and try to find a way to fulfill that need. Or, better yet, they would try to come up with a new game or toy to invent just for fun.

2

How Do I Turn My Ideas into Inventions?

BOBBY WENT TO HIS FATHER with a serious question. After he and Sally had visited her Uncle Edward, Bobby really wanted to invent something. He remembers Uncle Edward saying that to get ideas for inventions; a person had to look for a need and then try to solve that need.

"Dad, I have been looking for ideas to invent something. I started with my room and noticed several things I might invent to make keeping my room clean and organized a lot better," Bobby said. (Bobby was an unusual boy who liked to keep his room clean.)

"Well, did you come up with anything?" his Dad asked.

"Actually, I got several ideas, but when I checked on the internet, someone else had already done what I was thinking about. Then something happened. Mom asked me to carry the laundry basket up to her bedroom. The closet door was open and I saw a canvas shoe rack hanging on the back of the door. An idea popped into my head and I ran to call Sally. We both checked, but we could not find anything quite like my idea!" Bobby exclaimed.

"And what was that?" his Dad asked, wondering what kind of invention could be inspired by a shoe rack.

"Well, I noticed that Mom's shoe rack had rows of little pockets just big enough to slip a shoe inside. It was very handy. She could see which shoes she wanted at a glance. With just a little change, my invention would be perfect!" Bobby said excitedly.

"How will your invention work" his Dad asked.

"It will be like Mom's shoe rack, except mine will have wider pockets with only a little opening at the top of each pocket. The pockets will be just the size to slip in a video game disc.

Sally suggested the pockets be made out of clear plastic so we could see which game we wanted. The door rack will hold 4 discs across in six rows down. I can keep twenty-four games right at my fingertips!" Bobby explained.

His Dad thought a while before asking, "Have you figured out how much material you will need, how the rack will hang on the door, and how much it is all going to cost?"

"I'm way ahead of you, Dad. Grandma came over and we measured the door. She told me how much canvas and plastic she'll need to sew it up for me. Then we talked about reinforcing trim and the metal eyelets and hooks needed to hang it up on my door. I have plenty of money saved up from the odd jobs I've done in the neighborhood and my birthday presents to buy every-thing I need. Sally is going to get her Dad to advise us about the hardware we'll need, and she wants to pay for that out of her sav-ings."

Bobby and Sally were very happy. They had discovered a need and invented a way to fill that need, just like Uncle Edward had suggested. By the following afternoon, both of them had their video game and movie disc racks hanging from their bedroom closet doors. They both had light gray canvas backs, but Grandma had used pink trim on Sally's and green trim on Bobby's.

Sally and Bobby called Uncle Edward to come over and look at their invention. "That's what I was telling you. Find a new way of doing something and then do it!" he said. He was very proud of his niece Sally and her friend Bobby.

3

What Does Problem Solving Have to Do with Inventing?

BOBBY AND SALLY were talking to their science teacher after school one afternoon. In class they had been discussing famous inventors like Thomas Edison and the Wright brothers. Sally asked a serious question. "When did inventing things begin?" she wanted to know.

"Well, Sally," Mrs. Craddock began, "have you ever heard the expression that necessity is the mother of invention?"

"Yeah, I've heard my Dad say that," Bobby said, "But I don't know what it means."

"Let's imagine back to the earliest human history," the teacher said, "and think about what they didn't have. Man wasn't

9

born with a spear in his hand. In fact, he was not as strong as many of the beasts around him. He was, in fact, way down on the food chain."

"It must have been awful," Sally said, "always trying to hide from large animals that wanted to make a meal of them."

"So you can see the need. Man saw that it was necessary to have some kind of weapon that could give him a chance against the animals," Mr. Craddock said.

"So they sharpened long poles to use as spears," Bobby suggested.

"Yes, but some animals had hides that were too tough for the wooden spears to penetrate. Then man noticed the natural flint, a type of rock, all around and realized that it could be shaped into cutting tools and sharpened for spear heads. If the wooden spears alone had been enough, do you think men would have ever thought about using flint to make spearheads and arrowheads?" Mrs. Craddock asked.

"I guess not, probably. If they did not need the flint weapons, why would they even think about them?" said Sally.

"Right. Now, can you think of other things men began to invent because they needed something they didn't have?" Mrs. Craddock asked.

"How about the wheel which was useful to move heavy things around?" Bobby suggested.

"And clay ovens to make cooking easier!" Sally expressed.

"Now look at more recent times in our history. What needs have produced inventions that we take for granted today?" the teacher urged her students.

"The light bulb! It was difficult to read at night with the dim glow of lanterns and candles!" Sally said excitedly.

"And cars!" Bobby added, "We needed better ways to get around instead of using horses for hauling and traveling."

"But some inventions like TV didn't come from any real need," Sally said.

"Yes, that's true. Mankind could get along without TV," Mrs. Craddock said, "but that invention did solve problems for us like having everyone aware of the important news of the day and providing cheap entertainment for our families."

"Some problems are very serious," Sally interjected, "My Mom says that when she was a girl polio was a scary problem and everyone was afraid. Then people like Dr. Jonas Salk found a way to solve that problem with a polio vaccine."

"Very good, Sally. So if you and Bobby want to become inventors, you should begin with something that is a problem for you and come up with a way to solve it," Mrs. Craddock said.

"My problem is having to eat broccoli," Bobby said with a glum expression, "but I don't know how I could invent something to solve that!"

4

Why Should I Keep My Ideas a Secret?

SALLY WAS VERY UPSET when she saw Bobby after class one day. She told Bobby how Tommy Winters had stolen her idea for a science project at the school spring fair.

"You shouldn't have told him what you were planning to do," Bobby said.

"But he's my friend!" Sally protested, "I never thought he would run home and get his Dad to help him build the project and bring it back to school first!"

"Let's go visit your Uncle Edward," Bobby suggested, "Maybe he can help you with a new idea for a science project."

Uncle Edward was happy to see his niece and her friend. He always enjoyed their visits and talking about inventions.

Sally, almost in tears, told her Uncle how Tommy had stolen her idea for the science fair. If she made hers now, it would look as though she had copied him!

"You have learned a very valuable lesson about keeping your ideas a secret until they can be established as your own. Let me give you an example. If I mention the name Galileo to you, what do you think of?" Uncle Edward asked.

"He's the guy who invented the telescope," Bobby answered.

"Wrong. He got the idea from a Dutchman named Hans Lippershey who actually invented the first telescope. Galileo set about building his own telescope using the Dutchman's idea and credit for the invention went to Galileo. Very few people today have ever heard of Hans Lippershey," Uncle Edward told the young students.

"Have you ever heard of Nikola Tesla?" Uncle Edward asked.

"We read about him briefly in school," Sally said, "I only remember that he worked for Thomas Edison and George Westinghouse."

"That's right. And many patents held by Edison and later by Westinghouse were probably Tesla's original ideas. Yet very few people today have ever heard his name," Uncle Edward said.

"I think I get what you're telling us, Sir," Bobby said, "If you have an idea for something like a science project or an invention, you should keep it secret until you are ready to put it on display for everyone to see. That way everyone will know it was all your idea."

"That's good thinking, Bobby, for things like science projects where there would be no time for someone to steal the idea and get it ready by an exhibition deadline. But for inventions, even more care must be taken. We don't have time today to discuss patents, but we will as soon as you come up with your own idea for something new to invent," Uncle Edward said.

"Well," said Sally, "while we've been talking, I've gotten a new idea for a science fair project that will blow Tommy's project out of the water!"

"Great! What is it?" Bobby asked.

"Bobby, you're my best friend, but I'm not telling *anybody* about this idea until I show it at the fair!" Sally exclaimed.

Bobby and Uncle Edward laughed. Sally had clearly learned the lesson about keeping good ideas a secret until the proper time to let everyone see the finished product.

5

How Can Inventing be Used as a Game?

ONE AFTERNOON DURING LAST PERIOD in school, Mrs. Craddock surprised her students by announcing that they would be playing a game in class. The children were very excited to find out what the game might be. Mrs. Craddock gave each student a brown paper bag and two sheets of poster paper. Inside the bags, each student found a wire coat hanger, some wire clippers and pliers, some duct tape, a small roll of twine, and some colored markers. Everyone wondered how these items might be used in a game.

"Class," Mrs. Craddock began, "We have been studying about famous inventors during the past few weeks. The game today is called 'The Inventing Game.' Using the materials given to you, I want each of you to invent something. It can be a useful object or something artistic for decoration. Let your imaginations run free as you look at the raw materials and decide what you will invent."

"Does it have to be something entirely new?" Bobby asked.

"No, it may be something that has already been invented but your invention is either a better or cheaper way to make the product. Many inventions are just improvements on old ideas," Mrs. Craddock explained.

Right away Bobby imagined how his raw materials could be fashioned into something he really needed. He had the habit of organizing his notes from his classes each day by entering them in files on his computer at home. Putting his notes flat on his computer desk made them difficult to see. He went right to work creating his note holder.

First, he cut his hanger into one long wire and began to mold it with his pliers. When he was finished, he had something that resembled an easel. Then he cut a piece of poster board to eight and a half by eleven inches. Using his duct tape, he fastened the board onto the easel. Next, he used some wire to make something like a large paperclip that he put on the top of the poster board. Taking a sheet of his notes, he clipped it to the easel. His new copy stand would make it much easier to read his notes while he entered them into his computer.

Sally invented a new board game she called *Graduation*. On a sheet of poster board she drew a snake like path divided into squares. In the some of the squares, she wrote different things like "You failed your test, go back two spaces," or "It's a school holiday, go forward one space," or "Caught cheating, lose a turn," or "You got an A, go ahead three spaces."

In one corner of the board, she drew a circle which she divided into four equal sections each painted a different color with the numbers 1, 2, 3, or 4 written on the colored wedges. She cut out an arrow and placed it in the center of the circle with a push pin. Players would then spin the arrow to see how far they could move on the board. The game pieces were different colored school books labeled with different school subjects. The object of the game was to arrive first at the square marked "Congratulations! You've graduated!"

Mrs. Craddock was very pleased with the different inventions, and the students all agreed that they learned something about inventing by playing their teacher's game.

6

Does My Invention Have to Look Good?

BOBBY AND SALLY took their inventions to show Uncle Edward. They were excited that he seemed to like their ideas for a class notes holder and a new board game. However, they had a question for their inventor friend.

"They don't look very professional," Sally moaned.

"No, but you get the idea from looking at them. These are just the beginning of your inventions. Do you know what these are called?" Edward asked.

"No. What *are* they called?" Bobby responded.

"They're called *prototypes*."

"Prototypes? What's that?" Sally wanted to know.

"Well, they are models of what you invented. These first models don't have to look professional. But before you send your ideas to a possible manufacturer, you might want to make better looking samples," Uncle Edward explained.

"Well, I can see how Sally could use better supplies and paints to make a more professional looking game, but look at mine! It's all wire, card board, and duct tape. I call it 'My Homework Helper,' but right now it looks more like a homework disaster. I could use it as it is, but I sure couldn't sell something that looks like this!" Bobby exclaimed.

Uncle Edward laughed. "Tell me, Bobby, how you imagine the real product to look. What materials would you like to use for the finished product?"

"I was thinking that plastic would be good. I could have four or five in different colors. But to make this in plastic I would need equipment I don't have. What can I do?" Bobby asked.

"There are several ways you might improve on your prototype, Bobby. Do you know what balsa wood is?"

"Oh, sure. I use it to build model airplanes," Bobby said.

"Well, you could use it to make your prototype. It's lightweight and easy to cut and carve. I can see how you would be able to improve the looks of your design to show a potential manufacturer. Many inventors have used wood models of their ideas to show the size and appearance of the invention. Others have used clay models, but I don't think that would work for your 'Homework Helper.' Today, though, there is another way to show your prototype. Come with me to my computer," Uncle Edward said.

At the computer he continued, "I have this program on my computer called a *cad*. That stands for *computer assisted drawing*. With this program, we can scan your existing prototype and then illustrate how it would look done in plastic. We can even turn it around for several views to show front, back, and sides."

"I've seen things like that on the internet and in video games!" Sally exclaimed, "I've often wondered how they do it."

"But what we end up with is just an illustration," Bobby moaned, "It's not really a prototype."

"True, but computer drawn prototypes are called *virtual prototypes*. I think a really good three dimensional illustration might be all that is necessary to show manufacturers your invention," Uncle Edward said. "Come back to my house this weekend, and I'll teach you how to do it."

Sally and Bobby left all excited, hardly able to wait for Saturday morning.

7

Will People Buy My Invention?

BACK IN MRS. CRADDOCK'S classroom, they were still studying about inventors. Mrs. Craddock began by telling the class that not all inventions became successes. Even great and well-known inventors had come up with ideas that did not catch on with the public. She suggested that they look at the inventions students had done last week.

"The question is, will people buy a new invention," Mrs. Craddock said. "Let's start with Sally's board game, *Graduation*."

Marcie Aiken raised her hand. "Well, it's a neat idea," she said, "but who plays board games anymore? Most of my friends are into video games they can even play on their cell phones.

Maybe my younger sister and her friends might enjoy it. They play board games sometimes."

"Well, *somebody's* buying them. At the department store there is a whole section of various board games," Gary Wilson said.

"So, you think Sally ought to try and sell her idea to a board game manufacturer?" Mrs. Craddock asked, "Do you think it will catch on?"

The class voted that Sally should present her idea and see what happened. Then they turned their attention to Bobby's 'My Homework Helper.' Now he had a virtual prototype (computer drawing) of his invention thanks to Uncle Edward.

Gary Wilson commented, "I wouldn't buy it. I don't have a computer, so it wouldn't be of any use to me."

"Well, I *do* have a computer," Marcie interjected, "and I can see how it would come in handy. When I have to write an essay, I make a written outline before I write my assignment on the computer. I think the 'Homework Helper' would come in very handy."

"I like the different color choices, too," Angie Markham added. "I'd like a red one to match my laptop!"

Most of the students in the class said that they had computers at home. Several of them mentioned that they like to keep their desks looking neat. Bobby's invention would look nice and keep them from having notes scattered all round while they worked. Their conclusion was that both Sally's and Bobby's inventions might be very successful.

"What makes a new invention catch on with the public so that almost everyone wants to buy it?" Mrs. Craddock asked.

"Sometimes it's just something unusual and fun," Sally said, "I have a blanket that has sleeves in it I use when watching TV or reading a book on a cold night. Almost all my friends have one, too. I think they caught on because they were novel ideas. I don't really need my blanket with sleeves, but it makes me happy to use it."

"Good advertising has a lot to do with it, too," Marcie said, "I've noticed that many items in stores now have signs that read, As Seen On TV. It always makes me remember the TV commercials and I usually stop to have a closer look."

To sum up their discussion about what makes an invention sell, the class made several observations. One, many inventions sell because they provide a better way of doing something. Two, others sell well because they look interesting and offer a certain degree of fun. Three, some become best sellers because they are well advertised.

What the class noticed, however, was that of the millions of inventions made each year only a few ever became commercial successes.

8

Inventing a Better Mousetrap

WALKING HOME FROM SCHOOL one afternoon, Bobby and Sally were talking about something Mrs. Craddock had said in class, "Build a better mousetrap, and the world will beat a path to your door." Her comment opened the door for a discussion about how inventing is not always about something new, but something better.

"Cars and light bulbs," Bobby said.

"What?" Sally asked, "What do you mean?"

"Well, take cars. If no one ever came up with better ideas, there wouldn't be radio in our cars or even air conditioning. Inventors looked at cars and began thinking of new ways to make them better," Bobby said.

"I get it! Today we have cars that even talk to us while we're driving, and some cars can even parallel park themselves," Sally said.

"So inventors began thinking of ways to make light bulbs better. Then after fluorescent bulbs were invented, another situation caused inventors to design light bulbs that use a lot less electricity," Bobby added.

"I guess our inventions are like that. My board game is nothing new except that it stresses education and motivates the players to graduate. It offers another objective instead of collecting play money," Sally said.

Bobby commented, "And mine is not really new at all except that it is designed for kids and has more color. So now we want to find out if the customers think we've built better mousetraps!" They had a good laugh out of that.

"Can you think of other inventions that were improvements on things already invented?" Sally asked.

"Well, look at video games. Dad showed me a ping pong video game he used to play when he was my age. It was black and white and has two small lines with a ball. Really boring. My latest game is in 3D with characters and settings like a Hollywood movie. Who knows what the next inventor will do with that!" Bobby suggested.

"And TV," Sally said, "my grandpa told me about the first TV he ever saw. It was in a big box with a small round black and white picture tube. He said the images were only in focus right in the center of the picture. Then someone figured out how to make the picture square, bigger, and sharper. Other inventors turned their attention to broadcasting color images. But the TVs were still large boxes with all kinds of tubes and wires inside. Now my family has a large screen plasma TV that is thin enough to hang on our den wall. We have all of that because inventors kept thinking about how TV could be improved."

"You know," Bobby said, "right now I can't think of a single invention that has not been improved on when someone had a better idea. I'm really beginning to see how inventors are some of the most important people in the world."

9

How Can I Protect My Invention?

JUST BEFORE SUMMER VACATION, Mrs. Craddock invited Uncle Edward to come and speak to the class. He was to tell the students how to protect their ideas and inventions. Sally glared at Tommy Winters and said she had learned the hard way not to share her ideas with anyone else before she got credit herself. She did not tell the class how Tommy had stolen her science fair idea.

"Before we sent Sally's idea for a new board game to possible manufacturers," Uncle Edward began, "we took the time to have manufacturers sign a *non-disclosure agreement* which is basically a promise not to tell anybody about Sally's idea. If a manufacturer likes her idea, we might even get a patent".

"What's a patent?" Gary Wilson asked.

"Well, a patent is a claim of ownership for an invention. It contains a full description of the invention and drawings of the invention and it is submitted to the United States Patent and Trademark Office (USPTO). Thomas Edison held over a thousand patents."

"Why is that necessary if you keep your invention a secret?" Sally asked.

Uncle Edward replied, "Suppose you have an idea and you tell all your friends. Anyone you tell about your idea can use it without being obligated to pay you a penny. After all your hard work, you wouldn't want simply to give away your idea, would you?"

"No!" the class all responded in unison.

"Is it difficult to get a patent?" Marcie asked.

"It's a little like studying for an exam," Uncle Edward said, smiling broadly, "It takes time and effort. Then it may take a long time at the patent office because of the large number of applications they receive. The patent office can either say yes or no on your patent."

"So you can't make and sell your invention until you get a patent, right?" Bobby asked.

"No, that's not right, Bobby. You are not required to ever get a patent to make and sell your ideas if you don't want one. However, if you do apply for a patent, once you've applied, your invention can be sold by labeling it 'Patent Pending.' That tells people that you are in the process of getting a patent so they better think twice before using your idea," Edward said.

10

How Can My Invention Make Money?

ALL THE TALK about inventing had Sally and Bobby thinking about making money from their ideas. In the discussion in the classroom, it appeared that Sally's board game and Bobby's 'Homework Helper' might not be appealing to some shoppers. Uncle Edward told them it was worth a try to offer the ideas to large companies that might be interested in producing their inventions.

Uncle Edward showed them how to collect a list of possible manufacturers and how to write a proposal to submit to them. After contacting the manufacturers, there was a long wait to hear back from them. When the first rejection letters arrived, Bobby and Sally were terribly disappointed, but Uncle Edward insisted that they keep trying with other companies.

Finally, near the end of the school year, Sally got a letter from a famous toy manufacturer that they accepted her idea and offered her a contract for a sum of money they proposed to pay her for the game. Sally's father and Uncle Edward took her to visit a lawyer who advised them on what to do. Sally and her father signed the contract and the toy company sent them a check that they deposited in Sally's college fund. It was a very exciting time.

Bobby's 'Homework Helper' did not fare so well. All of the possible manufacturers said approximately the same thing: Our market research indicates that there would be only a small percent of students who would purchase the 'Homework Helper'. Bobby was not discouraged, however.

"I'll come up with another idea," he told Uncle Edward. "I like inventing and I know one day I will make something that many people will want to have."

Uncle Edward showed Bobby his idea notebook that listed all of his inventions that never got made. "You see, Bobby, ideas you have that are quite good may not be something a company feels it can make money with. This other notebook lists all of my inventions that are on the market today. I have made good money with my ideas, Bobby, but what keeps me working is my love of inventing."

Bobby nodded his head. He had caught the inventing bug himself.

"Let me tell you a story from my youth," Uncle Edward said. "When I was a young boy, I used to listen to radio dramas and comedies. One of those was about an inventor. I remember one story where the inventor had created a spray that would make garments waterproof. He was sure he'd make a lot of money with his invention. But when he presented it to the manufacturer, he discovered that another inventor had come up with waterproof fabric that the company was using to make garments. The spray was out of date before it could get on store shelves.

"The point is that while we are inventing, someone else is inventing, too. We never know if our ideas will be first or best. Some of them will make money for us and others will be rejected. Money is nice, don't get me wrong, but the real thrill is inventing something new or better."

"Thanks, Uncle Edward," Bobby smiled, "I'm going home right now and think up a new invention!"

Kid Inventor Success Stories

LET'S LOOK AT A COUPLE of real life young inventors. We will give you just a few words about both of them. If you're interested, you can learn mare about them on the internet, but ask your parents first.

Chester Greenwood

Chester Greenwood was only fifteen years old when he invented something in 1873 that we still use today—ear muffs. He got his grandmother to help him with the sewing part of his invention. In 1877 he was awarded a patent for his invention and set up a factory where they made the useful winter apparel for nearly sixty years. He invented many other things and had several businesses over his lifetime.

Kathryn (KK) Gregory

KK was only ten years old in 1994 when she got an idea also inspired by cold weather. She noticed that while playing in the snow, there was a space between her gloves and the bottom of her jacket sleeves. This allowed her wrists to become very cold and uncomfortable. KK went inside and designed Wristies®, fingerless gloves to wear under mittens or gloves. The "wristie" covers the part of the arm not protected by gloves and jacket sleeves. KK patented and trademarked her invention and became the youngest person ever to sell a product on the television network QVC.

Top 10 Things to Remember About Inventing

1. Anyone can be an inventor, even you.

2. Identify a problem and try to solve it through inventing.

3. Keep your ideas a secret and tell only your family.

4. Inventions can be new ideas.

5. Inventions can be made when you make something better.

6. Inventions can change the world.

7. Inventions can make millions of dollars.

8. Coming up with ideas is free.

9. With time and effort, your invention might be sold in stores.

10. Inventing is something you can do your whole life.

The Big Idea Notebook Section

This section is the beginning of your Big Idea Notebook.

This is where you can write down and draw all of your amazing

ideas. Have fun!

Name of your invention: _____

The date of when you came up with your invention: _____

Name of your invention: _____

The date of when you came up with your invention: _____

Name of your invention: _____

The date of when you came up with your invention: _____

Name of your invention: _____

The date of when you came up with your invention: _____

Name of your invention: _____

The date of when you came up with your invention: _____

Name of your invention: _____

The date of when you came up with your invention: _____

Name of your invention: _____

The date of when you came up with your invention: _____

Name of your invention: _____

The date of when you came up with your invention: _____

Name of your invention: _____

The date of when you came up with your invention: _____

Name of your invention: _____

The date of when you came up with your invention: _____

Name of your invention: _____

The date of when you came up with your invention: _____

Name of your invention: _____

The date of when you came up with your invention: _____

Name of your invention: _____

The date of when you came up with your invention: _____

Name of your invention: _____

The date of when you came up with your invention: _____

Name of your invention: _____

The date of when you came up with your invention: _____

Name of your invention: _____

The date of when you came up with your invention: _____

Name of your invention: _____

The date of when you came up with your invention: _____

Name of your invention: _____

The date of when you came up with your invention: _____

Name of your invention: _____

The date of when you came up with your invention: _____

Name of your invention: _____

The date of when you came up with your invention: _____

Name of your invention: _____

The date of when you came up with your invention: _____

Name of your invention: _____

The date of when you came up with your invention: _____

Name of your invention: _____

The date of when you came up with your invention: _____

Name of your invention: _____

The date of when you came up with your invention: _____